For Jonah—L.G.
For my mom, with love—M.M.

Text copyright © 2002 by Laura Godwin
Illustrations copyright © 2002 by Mary Morgan Van Royen
For information address Hyperion Books for Children, 114 Fifth Avenue, New York, New York 10011-5690.
Printed in Mexico.
This book is set in Kennerley 30/36.
The artwork for each picture was prepared using watercolors and colored pencils.
First Edition
1 3 5 7 9 10 8 6 4 2
Library of Congress Cataloging-in-Publication Data
Godwin, Laura.
What the baby hears / Laura Godwin ; illustrated by Mary Morgan Van Royen.—1st ed.
p. cm.
Summary: Rhyming text reveals the loving sounds baby animals hear from their parents, from the "nuzzle, nuzzle, nuzzle" heard by the colt to "I love you" heard by a human baby.
ISBN 0-7868-0560-9 (trade) — ISBN 0-7868-2484-0 (library)
[1. Animal sounds—Fiction. 2. Parent and child—Fiction. 3. Animals—Infancy—Fiction. 4. Stories in rhyme.] I. Morgan Van Royen, Mary. 1957– ill. II. Title.
PZ8.3.G5465 Wh 2002
[E]—dc21
00-33516
Visit www.hyperionchildrensbooks.com

What the Baby Hears

Laura Godwin

Illustrated by Mary Morgan

Hyperion Books for Children
New York

What the
puppy
hears—

Lick, lick, lick

What the beetle hears—

Click, click, click

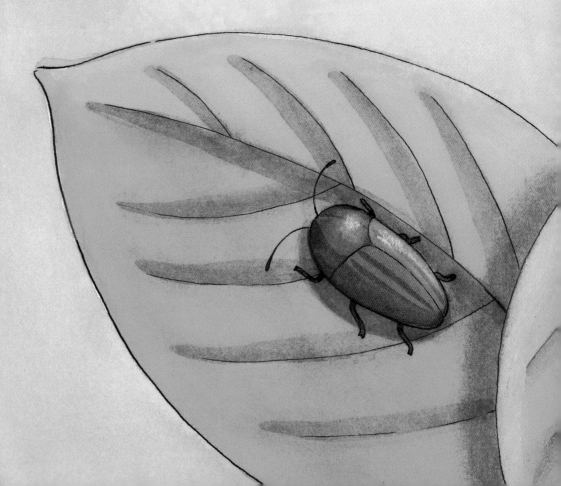

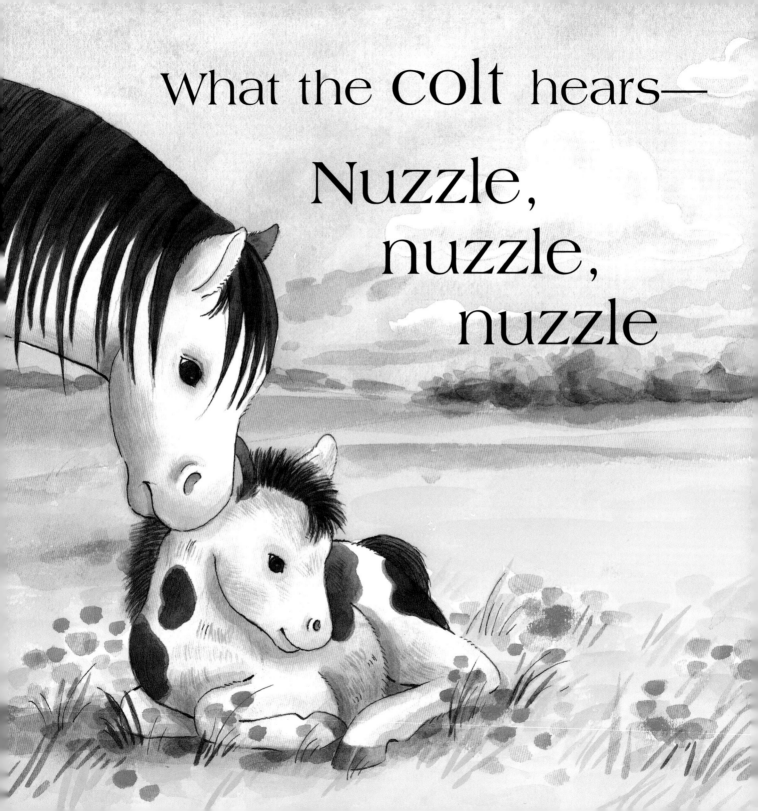

What the **colt** hears—

Nuzzle,
nuzzle,
nuzzle

What the **kid** hears—

Guzzle,
guzzle,
guzzle

What the piglet hears—
Oink, oink, oink

What the joey hears—

Boink,
    boink,
boink

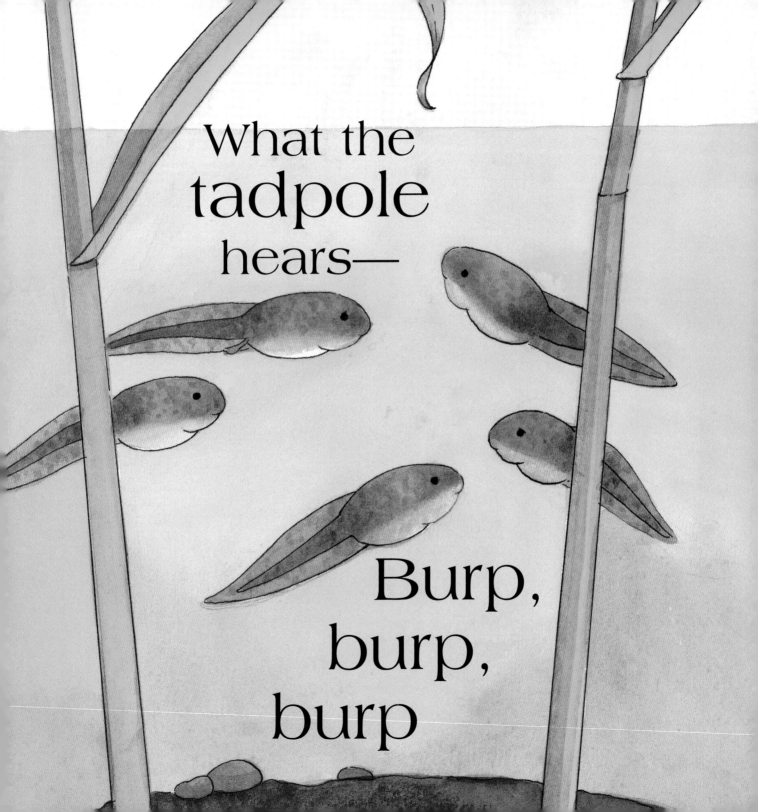

What the
tadpole
hears—

Burp,
burp,
burp

What the
robin
hears—

Chirp, chirp, chirp

What the bear cub hears—

Grrr, grrr, grrr

What the kitten hears—

Purr,
purr,
purr

What the OWLet hears—

Hoo,
hoo,
hoo

What the
baby
hears—

I love you!